PRAISE FOR M. L. BUCHMAN

Top 10 Romance of 2012, 2015, and 2016.

— BOOKLIST: THE NIGHT IS MINE, HOT POINT,
HEART STRIKE

One of our favorite authors.

— RT BOOK REVIEWS

Buchman has catapulted his way to the top tier of my favorite authors.

— FRESH FICTION

A favorite author of mine. I'll read anything that carries his name, no questions asked. Meet your new favorite author!

— THE SASSY BOOKSTER, FLASH OF FIRE

M.L. Buchman is guaranteed to get me lost in a good story.

— THE READING CAFE, WAY OF THE WARRIOR:
NSDQ

I love Buchman's writing. His vivid descriptions bring
everything to life in an unforgettable way.

— PURE JONEL, HOT POINT

THE CHRISTMAS LIGHTS OBJECTIVE

A NIGHT STALKERS 5E ROMANCE

M. L. BUCHMAN

Buchman Bookworks

Other works by M. L. Buchman:

<u>The Night Stalkers</u>
Main Flight
The Night Is Mine
I Own the Dawn
Wait Until Dark
Take Over at Midnight
Light Up the Night
Bring On the Dusk
By Break of Day
White House Holiday
Daniel's Christmas
Frank's Independence Day
Peter's Christmas
Zachary's Christmas
Roy's Independence Day
Damien's Christmas
and the Navy
Christmas at Steel Beach
Christmas at Peleliu Cove
5E
Target of the Heart
Target Lock on Love
Target of Mine

<u>Firehawks</u>
Main Flight
Pure Heat
Full Blaze
Hot Point
Flash of Fire
Wild Fire
Smokejumpers
Wildfire at Dawn
Wildfire at Larch Creek
Wildfire on the Skagit

<u>Delta Force</u>
Target Engaged
Heart Strike
Wild Justice

<u>Where Dreams</u>
Where Dreams are Born
Where Dreams Reside
Where Dreams Are of Christmas
Where Dreams Unfold
Where Dreams Are Written

<u>Eagle Cove</u>
Return to Eagle Cove
Recipe for Eagle Cove
Longing for Eagle Cove
Keepsake for Eagle Cove

<u>Henderson's Ranch</u>
Nathan's Big Sky

<u>Love Abroad</u>
Heart of the Cotswolds: England

<u>Dead Chef Thrillers</u>
Swap Out!
One Chef!
Two Chef!

<u>Deities Anonymous</u>
Cookbook from Hell: Reheated
Saviors 101

<u>SF/F Titles</u>
The Nara Reaction
Monk's Maze
the Me and Elsie Chronicles

<u>Strategies for Success (NF)</u>
Managing Your Inner Artist/Writer
Estate Planning for Authors

"This sounds as much fun as an air raid at Christmas… Wait, that's what it is." The guy in the goofy Santa hat cut Kelsey off after her opening line of the mission briefing: *This mission flies tonight.*

"Dashing through the air," the senior crew chief of the Night Stalker Chinook helicopter team began singing in her bright soprano. "In a two-rotor heli-sleigh."

"Over the jungle we go, a-fighting all the way," another joined in—an off-key tenor.

The various members of the operation's primary helicopter crew began adding in verses. Soon both pilots and three crew chiefs were rocking to the beat just as if they were in their massive, twin-rotor Chinook.

Sergeant Jason Gould—loadmaster on the *Calamity Jane II* and the man wearing the goofy Santa hat—joined in with a rich baritone. She didn't know why she should be surprised.

But she *was* surprised. He looked like a New York Jew from her own Brooklyn neighborhood. His speaking voice, while pleasant in the few words she'd been willing to exchange with someone in a Santa hat, hadn't foreshadowed the bone-melting baritone that quickly became the anchor of the song.

She could almost like him, except his hat sported a blinking-nose Rudolph on it. In her book, it was a target saying, "Please shoot me here." Though since they'd just met, and they were both US Special Operations, she left her sidearm in its holster.

They sat in a meeting room in the team's residence building. It stood beside a large hangar—labeled as abandoned. Abandoned deep in the woods of Fort Rucker, Alabama. She'd been directed down a tiny access road that was marked as closed and had looked disused. The gray afternoon, dripping with December rain, made both the building and hangar appear even more sad and weather-beaten. She'd almost turned around—until she noticed the cutting-edge surveillance and security system tucked in the corners of the structures.

The inside of the residence, once she'd gained admittance, was immaculate and comfortable with all of the latest conveniences. She hadn't seen the inside of the hangar yet.

The meeting room's walls were covered in brilliant travel posters—so many of them that they were starting to overlap: Costa Rica, Honduras, and Venezuela were understandable. But there was also Afghanistan, Iraq, Somalia, Libya…

It was the strangest briefing room décor Kelsey Killaney had ever worked in.

"It's my Christmas, too. Not my call." She grimaced as her protest cut off the singing. *Killjoy Killaney.* Once again, the old high school nickname was definitely her. If it *had* been up to her, she'd have scheduled the flight for Christmas Eve anyway, just so that she didn't have to think about "the happy season" for one more millisecond than necessary. But it had been circumstances, not orders that had brought them together on Christmas Eve afternoon.

This morning, everyone at her office in Fort Belvoir, Virginia had been buzzing with the "Best Wishes" and merry yeah-whatever. She'd wanted to lie on the floor and throw a tantrum as if she was nine, not twenty-nine—the little girl wanting everyone to just shut up. Her worldview was more mature now. Now, she was a grown woman who just wished everyone would go away.

Another Christmas wish gone bust. Not that any of the ones as a child had paid off.

This morning, Michael Gibson, the commander of Delta Force, had appeared at her desk inside The Activity's headquarters without warning—not even from security who were there to make sure such things didn't happen. The Intelligence Support Activity worked in one of the most secure buildings on a fort made up of twenty major intel agencies. The Activity's sole purpose was serving the Special Operations Forces, but that didn't mean they were supposed to be able to just walk in.

"There's a jet waiting for you at Davison Army Airfield," had been his idea of a pleasant Christmas Eve morning greeting—which actually worked for her. "Here's your team and mission file to read on the flight."

He'd handed her a slim folder that she wanted to handle as much as a live snake. It had a yellow fly sheet with a dark red border. In large type it only had an identification number and two of the scariest words in the intelligence business: Eyes Only. She'd checked the back of the fly sheet. Her name had been added in the second position, countersigned by Colonel Michael Gibson himself. Theirs were the only two names on the file.

She'd looked back up at him, but he'd been gone. If not for the file clutched in her white-knuckled fingers, she'd have doubted he'd ever been there. One look at the first page and she was on the move. On her way out the door to grab the scram kit from the trunk of her car, she'd stopped off at the front desk. Just as she suspected, he never *had* been signed in…or even seen—Delta Force guys were just creepy sometimes.

Reading the mission portion of the file Gibson had given her, made her the obvious choice for the operation. Actually, the only choice.

Reading the portion about the 5E was just…headshaking.

The 5E had an unprecedented number of missions with an unlikely success rate—even by the Night Stalkers' stratospheric standards. Yet the details of most of their missions had been redacted from the file now sitting in the locked briefcase at her feet.

With their song cut off, they were all sitting and waiting. Waiting and ready for their latest mission assignment. That's when she looked at the posters again.

"Duh!"

Jason, happy in his Santa hat, looked over but she just shook her head to ward him off. She hoped he would look away before she was forced to attack Rudolph's blinking nose. The last thing she needed was to explain herself to a Night Stalking Christmas elf, no matter how nice a voice he had. Why was a New York Jew singing Christmas carols anyway?

Except he wasn't a fellow Brooklynite. According to the file, Loadmaster Jason Gould was from Florida no matter how much he sounded New York.

Kelsey understood now. She didn't need the list of redacted missions—they were right there on the walls. These people collected travel posters of everywhere they'd ever had an operation. Now she could start putting some of the pieces together.

Each poster was a snapshot of a mission file.

"Find Beauty in Honduras." A black ops Honduran

mission last year that had shaken the corrupt banking-military cooperative to the core. It had significantly stabilized the duly-elected government—but no hint of who had done the mission. The answer sat in this room.

"Surf Kamchatka." The 5E had done the Russian drone mission.

"Hike the Negev." The disastrous Negev Desert, Israel, mission that had shaken The Activity itself to the core, somehow salvaged by the field team. By this team.

She tried to catch her breath, but wasn't having much luck. No wonder she hadn't heard of the 5E, though they were the logical extension of Henderson's and Beale's D Company. The 5D had been hugely innovative in their approach to military tactics. The 5E, however, were the tactical equivalent of Delta Force—silent and dangerous as hell…or Christmas.

"Damn it!" Jason complained. "Christmas Eve! Shit, man! And I was going to get my nails done tonight." That earned a laugh around the table. The team was apparently unflappable.

Despite her clumsiest efforts, their spirits remained high.

She got along with data, not people.

Activity agents were rarely in on the final mission. They might go out into the field a dozen times themselves gathering intelligence, but operations were generally left to the action teams. But tonight there was no choice.

Kelsey couldn't stop herself from glancing down at Sergeant Jason Gould's hands as he made a show of inspecting his nails critically. They were cut short, uneven, and showed that he made his living with those hands—which made sense for a ramp gunner on an MH-47G Chinook. As one of the three crew chiefs, he'd have a dozen roles to serve—all of which said competent and strong. He was several inches taller than her own five-seven with an attractive leanness. She knew from his file that his family had a sportfishing business out of St. Petersburg, Florida. Curly dark hair and nearly black eyes.

She'd almost been attracted—if not for her hopelessness with attractive men. And the stupid hat.

"We'll go together, Jason. I need a mani-pedi anyway." Carmen. Dark red hair. Crew chief of the Chinook. Married to the co-pilot on the same craft. What a crazy outfit.

Five aboard the Chinook and four more aboard each of the two DAP Hawk gun platforms that would be flying protection. With her that made a total of fourteen flying tonight, plus two assets who had yet to arrive.

As Kelsey had no more control over the crew selection than the mission, she started the briefing. They might appear carefree, but the moment she began laying out the details of the mission, she had a hundred percent of their attention.

CHAPTER 2

It was still mid-afternoon by the time the short briefing ended and they were into the hangar. The soft rain had turned downright wet.

Jason had been searching for an excuse to talk to Kelsey Killaney since the moment she'd hit the pavement at the 5E's compound. He found it when they stepped into the hangar.

"Stealth, ma'am. Every last bird." Their big Chinook, two DAP Hawks—Black Hawks turned into the world's most advanced gun platforms, and two Little Birds. The last wouldn't be on this mission, and the crews hadn't been called.

"I see that," she sounded a little breathless. "I've simply never heard of them."

"Must admit that we like it that way."

"It explains how," she looked at him puzzled for a moment, as if surprised to find herself talking to him. "How you do what you do."

"That, and the best crew flying." He still couldn't believe that he was here. He supposed it was just being in the right place at the right time. After the Negev Desert disaster, they'd needed a new bird. The Army had provided them with the stealth configured *Calamity Jane II* and shipped them down to the 5E's team at Fort Rucker. Their mission pace had doubled and the complexity as well. He'd always simply been glad to be flying, but in the 5E he'd become more than he'd ever imagined.

And now, with Kelsey Killaney standing so close beside him that he could smell her fresh scent, like a strange winter flower, he started to understand just what he'd achieved. He was a goddamn flyer on the best bird in the sky, anywhere. Maybe, just maybe, he was good enough to stand next to a woman like her and not feel out of place.

They were following the rest of the crew up the rear ramp of the *Calamity Jane II*, prepping it for the first leg of the flight.

Her light brown hair was back in a severe ponytail that emphasized her large eyes. She was fair-skinned and had one of those smiles that looked as if it was always ready, even though she hadn't used it yet that he'd seen. The fact that she worked for The Activity said she was screamingly intelligent —an assumption borne out by the concise style of her briefing. If smart was the new sexy, she was a chart breaker— not that she wasn't by the old measure as well.

He'd truly done his best to pay attention at the briefing, but it had been hit and miss. He'd managed to sit next to her, by the simple stratagem of holding out a chair for her. But, no matter what he did, he couldn't get her to laugh. That hint of a smile hadn't even shifted when he'd started a whole riff about personal grooming tips off Carmen's mani-pedi remark—which was more Zoe the drone pilot's thing than Carmen's anyway.

Danny and the Captain were already in their seats running through checklists. Carmen and George were still outside pulling off pitot tube and air intake covers. So he had a moment and intended to use every second of it to his advantage.

"You need anything, ma'am? If so, I'm your man." He tried not to wince. Smooth as descending staircase on a tricycle—a trick he'd only tried once, but possibly where he got his taste for flying. He was getting no points for subtlety on this effort.

"Do you have a reality check somewhere?" Her question caused him to do a doubletake. So she did have a sense of humor behind her ever-so-serious facade.

"Somewhere, sure." Jason began patting the pockets of his flightsuit, peeked inside a couple of the pouches on his survival vest, and finally pulled a small pack of candy out of his medical supplies. "Will these do?"

Her expression turned into a dangerous scowl, "Hell no!"

He looked down to see if he'd mistakenly pulled out a grenade or a breaching charge, but he hadn't. "Who doesn't like Skittles?"

She sighed and rested a hand on his arm a moment as if apologizing.

Her fingers were almost delicate, but he could see a strength to them. She was so fit that he'd have guessed she was the sort who went to the high-end gym three times a week with a gaggle of girlfriends and had an impossibly handsome aerobics trainer named Julio—*except* that she was Activity. The agents from The Activity were just as likely to go into the field to gather their own intel from behind enemy lines as they were to work at a desk in Fort Belvoir. They were known for being ruthlessly competent. Another thing he liked in a woman. If competence was the new sexy, then—

"Thanks for the offer and, yes, I do like Skittles. I just have this thing about Christmas, so thanks but no thanks."

He looked down at the little pack. It was clearly labeled

Holiday Mix and showed only red and green flavors rather than the normal rainbow.

"Seems like you're putting a lot of weight on a little bit of seasonal packaging."

She nodded, "No argument from me. It's the one topic I'm a complete lunatic on."

"Christmas?"

"Christmas," she confirmed as if it was an incursion by an entire battalion of Taliban.

"Completely rational about everything else?"

"Everything!" Kelsey's tone was dry enough for him to laugh, which had several of the crew turning to look at him.

He squinted at Carmen, who had just come aboard and was checking over the internal systems, and mouthed, "What?"

Carmen shook her head, keeping her thoughts to herself, as she continued the pre-flight check.

Fine!

He tried to turn to give Carmen the cold shoulder, but she gave him an I-caught-you wink that blew his timing, even if he didn't know what she was on about.

"Even rational about men?" Jason turned back to Kelsey.

"Always," then she grimaced, "for what good it has ever done me."

"I'm not sure if I should ask if that's a good sign or a bad one for me."

"As long as you're wearing that hat? Bad sign."

He looked up enough to spot the white, furry trim just above his eyebrows and remembered the blinking Rudolph.

"Nope," he looked back down at her and made a point of shaking his head hard enough to make the little bell at the end tinkle brightly. "Even being a gorgeous Activity agent, I'm not giving up my hat for you."

"Your loss," and finally that smile of hers came out. She

did a quick turn and hair toss worthy of any disdainful supermodel, then strode up the cargo bay. But it was the smile that slayed him. From pretty to radiant faster than a heat-seeking missile.

He could only wonder what it would take to make her smile like that again. Taking off his hat? No. She'd smiled while making a joke because he had it on. He'd stick with a winning hand, no matter what she said about Christmas.

There had to be a reason behind it, but he wasn't sure how comfortable he felt digging for it with a complete stranger, no matter how attractive. It wasn't just her beauty. Something in her drew him—deeply. Not a feeling he was used to.

Done with the exterior inspection, George boarded as well and began checking his Minigun just as Carmen began going over hers. His own M240 hung out of the way in its bracket close by the rear ramp.

Kelsey sat in the observer's chair just behind the pilots' seats. That should be safe, they were both married: the Captain to the unit's hot Italian drone pilot and quiet Danny —impossibly—to the vivacious Carmen. The only other crew member was the portside gunner and George was too British to try poaching where Jason had showed interest.

Out of excuses, Jason started his own preflight checks of the *Calamity Jane II* for a mission. Ammo full-stocked after the last mission was still fully stocked. Emergency supplies of food, water, and first aid were fully stocked and inside the refresh date. Enough to feed the whole crew for a week if they went down hard somewhere.

Then he started in puzzling on Kelsey. She must have her own reasons for being so *Bah Humbug!* But it didn't fit her. She seemed...happier than that.

Quiet. Which among the screaming extroverts of the 5E must be a shock. But there was something more. As if—

A high whine of fast-moving tires was all the warning he had to dodge out of the way before a pair of Polaris MRZRs came racing up the rear ramp. He jumped aside, clinging to the inside of the Chinook's hull to stay clear. The MRZRs were four-seater ATVs on Special Operations steroids. Tough, lightweight, fast, electric-quiet, and able to carry a thousand pounds of soldier and gear at sixty miles an hour or scramble over rough terrain at twenty. Except instead of the usual Army tan, they'd been painted like blue and red hotrods. Blinking Christmas lights had been wound around the bars of the roll cage which didn't make much sense unless…undercover as civilian hotrod dune buggies.

Right. Low profile mission. But had the woman who hated Christmas thought of the Christmas lights? Jason suspected that she was the sort of woman who thought of everything and left nothing to chance.

The way the MRZRs raced aboard told him it was either SEAL or Delta at the helms.

Once they were in, he dropped back down. Both drivers wore clip-on fuzzy antlers.

"Duane? Dude! Haven't seen your ugly face since you left the Rangers for that wimp-ass Delta outfit." They'd stayed in close touch, but in four years had never managed to be in the same place at the same time.

"Jason, you Night Stalker piece of shit!" They thumped each other's backs hard enough to hurt.

"Cool antlers. Too bad they aren't half as cool as my hat." Then he spotted the gorgeous Latina stepping out of the other rig. She looked *very* cute in her antlers.

"You must be Sofia. I can't believe that you fell for a lump of coal like this one."

"He is all mine," she said in a happy, lushly Spanish accent, as she gave him a hug. "I have heard so many good things about you. I would know you anywhere by your so very silly hat."

"And if it hadn't been Christmas?"

"By your *very* good looks," she didn't hesitate to laugh.

Then she turned to Duane but kept an arm around Jason's waist so he kept his around her shoulders.

"I do not know," Sofia said thoughtfully. "Jason is *so* handsome. Why didn't you ever tell me this. Maybe I should be with a Night Stalker man and not a Delta boy."

With all the speed Jason would expect of a Delta operator, Duane hip-checked him into the emergency fire extinguishing system and separated Sofia with a quick hand about her waist—a move so smooth that it had all three of them laughing.

CHAPTER 3

Kelsey sat at the far end of the helicopter's shadowed cargo bay and tried to look away. What would she give to be a part of that laughing circle of three? They looked so easy together, so effortlessly happy. That was a part of working for The Activity—she and the other analysts were a collection of loners, brought together by a fascination for the intricacies of information and an ability to turn it into actionable intelligence.

The folder that Colonel Gibson had provided was a perfect example. The first page had contained just three lines of information that suddenly brought her last six months of work into sharp focus.

Delta Team and 160th SOAR 5E, Ech Stagefield, Fort Rucker
Juan Zavala, Christmas Eve
(and an address in Cozumel)

IT WAS Christmas Eve Day and Colonel Gibson had given her the first actionable lead on the elusive Juan Zavala that she'd seen in six months of hunting for him.

Zavala was one of the kingpins of the ultra-violent Jalisco New Generation cartel that she'd been tracing. The Jalisco were the former armed wing of the Sinaloa cartel and were rapidly gaining precedence in the Mexican drug scene. Under the kingpin theory of "take out the top and the internecine battles will do the rest of the cleanup," Zavala was a prime target.

She even recognized the address. It was a beach house that she had researched as one of his likely safe houses, but had never been able to trace him to.

Then the woman separated herself from the two men as they turned to arranging the two MRZRs more carefully and tying them down for flight. She moved through shadows until she was almost at Kelsey's side.

"Sofia?" She'd never expected to see Sofia Forteza again since she had left The Activity.

"Kelsey!" And Sofia gave her a hug as well which surprised her completely. Sofia had been one of her few friends at The Activity before she'd made the unlikely shift to Delta Force. But they'd never had a hugging kind of friendship.

"You seem happy."

"Ecstatic! I didn't know how much I loved being out in the field. Actually, I did know that. I know it better now. And Duane certainly helps," she was practically glowing as she aimed a happy look back down the bay.

"How do you know Jason?" Kelsey wasn't sure why she was asking. She'd watched them hug and felt... She didn't know. As if she wished it was her instead?

"I don't. It is the way that Duane talked about him, I seem

to already know him. They served in the US Rangers together. They've stayed very close."

Another skill Kelsey didn't have. She'd lost touch with Sofia the moment she'd headed over the horizon.

"Is this mission yours?" Sofia's effortless manners didn't give Kelsey enough time to feel uncomfortable.

She nodded.

"Good," Sofia nodded her head emphatically in return as the APU screamed to life and then the twin turbines began spinning up. "Then I know everything will go fine."

"You do?" Kelsey must have heard wrong over the building noise. A backwash of hot exhaust rippled through the cabin—it would clear as soon as they were moving. She'd been worrying about the mission every second since Colonel Gibson had handed her the file then evaporated or dropped through a trap door or whatever he'd done.

Sofia dug into her pocket and pulled out a pair of earplugs as the engine noise escalated. She shouted as she slid them in. "You were always the best planner we had when the terribles hit the fan. Except for me, of course. We all knew it and it made you a little scary to work with."

"I was?"

Past words, Sofia simply nodded before heading back down to rejoin the men.

People were scared of her?

Actually, that explained some reactions she'd observed. Rooms did seem to go quiet when she stepped into them, as if she was checking up on everybody. Except the 5E's briefing room. They were so skilled that maybe nothing daunted them.

What would it be like to work with them more? On occasion, an agent was permanently embedded with an elite team to facilitate operational communications more tightly with The

Activity's specialties regarding human and signal intelligence. To be embedded with the 5th Battalion E Company would be both a challenge and…fun. Fun? That wasn't something she was very good at and erased the thought from her mind.

But she couldn't help glancing back down the cargo bay. Jason in his blinking Rudolph hat hadn't been afraid of her—just the opposite. He'd continued talking to her even after she'd snapped at him for offering her Christmas candy. Killjoy strikes again.

CHAPTER 4

*K*elsey Killaney's plan sounded simple on the surface. Jason now knew that the surface appearances had nothing to do with one of Kelsey's plans.

She'd only outlined the basic approach strategy back at Fort Rucker: length of flights, refueling stops, necessary equipment. Per her instructions, beneath his flightsuit he wore slacks, a dress-shirt, and running shoes, though she hadn't explained why at the time. Under his shirt he wore a vest of lightweight Dragonskin armor for a bit of invisible protection.

She'd laid it out on the four-hour flight down to Naval Air Station Key West and refined it on the three-hour crossing to Cozumel after they'd eaten a hurried dinner while refueling. He'd never been to the small resort island off the Yucatan coast. Bringing a hot babe down here for a winter vacation had definitely been on his bucket list.

He'd never imagined that when he did it, he'd be unloaded after nightfall onto an empty stretch of beach ten miles across the island from the city of San Miguel de Cozumel. The weather was perfect. They'd left the storm somewhere over the Florida Keys and now drove out beneath a canopy of stars. Shirt sleeves were just right for the warm evening, though he could have done without the extra layer of the Dragonskin.

Night Stalkers usually didn't deploy on the active part of the mission, that's what Ranger door kickers and Delta operators were for. His job was to get them there, then shuffle away and hide until it was time to come fetch them.

Not on a Kelsey Killaney mission.

"I need an expert in flight operations on the mission team in case something goes wrong."

He'd considered arguing, until she said she was going as well.

"There isn't time to sufficiently brief everyone on the layout. We only have tonight, so I have to be there. I've spent too long hunting Zavala to let him slip away."

Which explained why she'd only requested two Delta operators rather than a full team.

"Can you drive?" Kelsey had asked as they were releasing the tie-downs on the vehicles.

"Sure." Of course he could.

"I mean really drive?"

"Dad ran sprint car races for a hobby. If he paid the entry fee, then got a sportfishing client, I'd drive the race for him. I was a much better driver than I was a fisherman." Then he climbed into the driver's seat of the MRZR and buckled in to settle the point. An MRZR was a close relative of a sprint car. Four seats instead of one, no airfoil on the top, and an MRZR had an engine that could only go sixty, not a hundred and sixty. But those were the differences. In common, they both had: an open metal frame with a serious roll cage, a very low center of gravity, demon-like cornering abilities, and were made for running in the sand and dirt and being fast while doing it.

In the far back, an MRZR had an extra space like a miniature pickup. It could carry two extra soldiers or a pile of gear. Right now, they had massive tourist drink coolers—coolers that were loaded with all of their tactical gear and most of the weapons they had just illegally smuggled into a friendly country. Due to corruption, the results on these types of missions were often better if the foreign government wasn't notified. The challenge was to not be caught in the process as that tended to upset them badly.

It was only as they rolled off the back of the Chinook and onto the deserted beach, that the truth clicked in.

"You already knew that I could really drive. That's why you didn't get a second driver for this mission from Delta."

"Maybe I just like your hat," Kelsey said it as if she was all innocence. No, she said it like a tease—like maybe the first tease she'd ever made.

He drove up the beach and over the berm onto the Quintana Roo road, then waited for Duane and Sofia to join them in the second MRZR. How had that lucky bastard gotten a woman like that? Sofia was beyond beautiful, right up there in Kelsey Killaney's category. And she was a Delta Force fighter. As far as he knew, they had like three women in the entire unit, yet somehow Duane had won her heart. And not just a little. Married if that didn't beat all. The only man less likely to get married in their Ranger platoon than one Jason Gould.

That got Jason thinking about why he himself was that way. Because he was stupid? Or because he'd never met the right woman? He'd take answer B any day. Any day before now. He wasn't sure why she fascinated him so much, but that was a question he was willing to pursue.

"You hate my hat," he reminded her.

"You're right. I hate your hat."

"And how important is it that we go low profile undercover here?"

"Why do you think we repainted the MRZRs in hotrod colors and are wearing civilian clothes?"

"But you hate my hat."

She glared over at him.

"That's too bad." He wasn't quite sure why he'd grabbed the extra accessory when getting civilian clothes out of his room, but he had.

"Why? Because you so *love* your hat?"

"I do, but that's not the problem," he tried to shake his head as if she was pitiful.

Duane and Sofia cleared the berm and pulled up beside them on the empty highway as the helos disappeared back into the night: the big Chinook and the two guardian DAP Hawks. They'd fly out well beyond radar range and refuel from a circling C-130 tanker while they waited.

"Then what's the problem, Jason?" Kelsey's guard was down just enough that if he was quick…

He pulled out his second hat, triggered the flashing nose, and pulled it onto her head. Her hair was impossibly sleek, so smooth it might have been ice, but was so warm and human that it seemed to burn his hand. He yanked his hands away before he could do more.

"There," he declared. Stomping on the gas, he unleashed the MRZR. It leapt down the road with Duane and Sofia close behind. "Now you're low profile."

"I'm going to have to kill you, Jason," she shouted over the racing wind.

"Wait until after the mission, okay?"

CHAPTER 5

Kelsey tugged the hat down against the speed-generated wind and hated herself for it. Hated that she hated Christmas. Hated that she still didn't know how to be nice to Jason when he'd been nothing but nice to her. Wearing his stupid matching hat was the first concession she'd managed.

He looked over and grinned at her as he turned left onto the Carretera Transversal to cross the island.

"So, tell me why you're irrational about Christmas?" He shouted over the wind noise. The electric MRZR itself was quiet, but there was roaring wind and the tire noise as they raced the 9.3 miles across the island in a vehicle with no windshield. The wide two-lane road ran straight as an arrow between two uninterrupted walls of green—their headlights well-focused on the road ahead so that they'd be hard to spot from any distance.

Not a chance. "Tell me why you're so crazy for it that you have not one but two Rudolph hats."

They covered a mile in silence before he spoke. He slowed a little, but the road noise barely changed.

"Mom bought them for Dad and I last Christmas. This one is his," he tapped his forehead. "You're wearing mine."

"Why do you have *his* hat? Thief!" She was suddenly very conscious of having Jason's hat on her head. It was so… personal. As if they were together—somehow a couple.

Again the mile-long pause.

"The cancer killed Dad by Valentine's Day. Mom followed him, of a broken heart by July Fourth."

Kelsey felt as if she'd just been punched. She reached out and clamped a hand over his arm in sympathy. Could feel his muscles rippling beneath the surface as he drove. His strength a comfort, when she should be the one providing that.

"Sorry," he steadfastedly stared ahead without a glance toward her. "It just slips out sometimes. When I'm not being careful."

Kelsey could only look at him in amazement. His ridiculous hat and teasing her about it had more meaning than should be possible. In an instant he transformed from a ridiculous man who had been kind to her, to a kind man who didn't mind being perceived as ridiculous—even if he wasn't.

How was he so comfortable in his own skin that he could do that?

She was on the verge of asking, but knew that wasn't right. He'd just laid his heart out on the cross-Cozumel road. His honesty demanded the same.

"My parents hated each other. I still don't know why they stayed together."

Kelsey's hand still rode lightly on Jason's forearm, but she was reluctant to take it away. Through it, she could feel a listening stillness come over him.

"But they didn't fight all year. Instead, they saved all of their bitterness for one 'special season'," she wished she could do this softly rather than shouting it in short choppy sentences with no ability to gauge her listener's reaction. "The Christmas tree. Mom thinks they're pretty. Dad hates them as a waste of money, space, time… I don't know. It's not like we were poor. Maybe he hates them because Mom likes them. Dad would pick the fight starting in October. Stretch it into February when he was on a roll."

Jason's stillness continued as the lights of San Miguel de Cozumel city began to light the road ahead of them.

"Christmas is nothing but bad memories."

Jason slowed as they entered the outskirts of the city. He hadn't said a word as she'd told him something that she'd never told anyone. She'd always managed to keep her *Bah Humbug!* to herself before. Somehow was never dating anyone when Christmas came around, always opting out of Secret Santa at work. She'd stressed herself into actual illness before any number of Christmas parties.

And Jason just drove.

"Look."

She was looking, to see what his reaction to her was. For some reason it seemed to matter, but she couldn't read it.

Then he nodded to either side of the road.

She looked. There were breaks in the trees. Houses that were little more than hovels were tucked in among palm and avocado trees. And each one had bright Christmas lights. Sometimes just a doorway, sometimes a spiral climbing a palm tree, and frequently a lit creche of the birth in the manger in gaudy plastic. The closer they got to town, the more extravagant the displays.

They turned southwest on the Avenida Rafael E. Melgar.

The waterfront was a wonder of lights. To her right lay the sea. Cruise ship docks jutted out into the dark ocean— the ships lit like cities of their own. Hundreds and hundreds of people strolled along the seawall. Most holding hands or in close groups chattering happily together.

The street was divided by a narrow median with a palm tree every hundred feet or so, and each was brightly wound in Christmas lights. The one- and two-story whitewashed shops along the inland side of the street were a bounty of Christmas displays.

Jason continued to drive in silence.

People waved at them in their two colorfully lit MRZRs, dressed up so that they looked like high-end dune buggies. She waved back.

They passed a tall lighthouse close by the cruise terminal. It cast no light. Yet even from here, in the brightest heart of the promenade, she could see the tall beacon to the south that had replaced it—two white flashes every five seconds.

Was that herself? A decommissioned lighthouse amidst an abundance of light?

She turned back to Jason as he continued easing along in the southbound traffic. Was he the beacon that now flashed so brightly ahead? Somehow he was holding onto the joy that his dead parents had taught him while she was still wrapped up in the darkness that her parents had tried to teach her.

It was a crappy metaphor, especially if it was true and she was the decommissioned lighthouse.

Up ahead there was another light, far taller and flashing brightly. That looked like a much happier metaphor, if she could figure out how to live it.

CHAPTER 6

"I don't want to feel decommissioned any more." Kelsey slipped her hand off his arm and he missed it. He missed the comfort. He missed the connection.

"What?" Jason wondered where that had come from. He was still trying to shake off the memories of last Christmas, his dad already past being able to speak, but smiling as he wore his goofy hat. Meager presents opened on a hospital bed because no one could find the energy to shop for more.

"The lighthouses," Kelsey pointed upward.

Jason hadn't even noticed them. He could barely see anything other than the withered man who took up so little space on the vast bed.

"You think you're a decommissioned lighthouse?"

"Can't prove otherwise by me."

He'd heard her story, about her idiot parents. Had they somehow pounded into this beautiful woman's head that she wasn't worth better?

Jason had asked Sofia about her, when it was clear they knew each other.

"Not much to tell. Brilliant, driven, the very best in very

tough crowd. But she really keeps herself to herself, if you understand what I am meaning. She never talks about anything outside of the missions. So it's not as if I'm giving anything away because neither will she."

But Kelsey just had. To him.

"Kelsey?"

"Uh-huh."

"How could you get something so completely wrong?"

"What? I know where Zavala is. I know the layout of the house. We are the perfect assets to do this fast and quiet." She was back on the mission, and she was right. They'd rolled past the flashing lighthouse, leaving behind traffic, another cruise terminal, and once more were into the outskirts of the rapidly disappearing town.

"There," she pointed. They dropped down onto the narrow shore road past the big resorts, the Chankanaab Beach Resort being the last of them. He had a quick glimpse of a quiet lagoon and thatched huts. It was the sort of place he'd imagined bringing a woman, though not with a load of weapons, rather with a bikini and a lot of time with nothing planned.

They continued south along the shore. The low beach and berm were usually close by, except when lush estates pushed the access road inland.

"Here," Kelsey pointed again.

He turned off into a vacant lot. It made a gap through the scrub trees and palms connecting the road to the beach. He stopped before they reached the sand. The electric MRZRs were silent and he could hear the gentle splash of the waves picked out in the headlights. He and Kelsey here, together. It was very easy to imagine.

Duane and Sofia rolled up quietly behind them, but Jason ignored them.

Instead, he turned to Kelsey. Her face was randomly lit by

the blinking Christmas lights on the roll cage. The shifting shadows made it hard to read her expression.

"It's Christmas Eve," he said, for lack of any better ideas.

"It is," she looked down at her folded hands.

"Got a present for you."

"Better than this hat?" Then he saw her bite her lower lip because she now obviously understood the importance of the hat. He'd only been teasing when he put it on her, but it had gained so much meaning in the last half hour.

"Well, okay, it's not *that* cool, but I'm making this up as I go."

She only nodded, but it was quick, accepting. Then she appeared to brace herself.

He dug in his pocket and pulled out the bag of Christmas Skittles, handing it across solemnly.

Kelsey stared down at it for a long time before taking it gently from his hands.

"To hell with your past," he told her. "To hell with mine. New beginnings. Though I figured I was safer to start small." It was also the only thing he had to give at the moment.

She looked up at him with her dark eyes so wide that they seemed to catch all of the colors of the Christmas lights at once.

Then she clutched the little packet of candy to her chest with both hands, and nodded for him to continue down the beach.

The plan was fiendishly simple—he wondered if all of Kelsey's plans were like that. If so, she absolutely belonged in the 5E. It was beyond stealth…it was cool! And so much better than the home invasion that was their backup scenario.

They drove the two Christmas-decorated MRZRs slowly down the beach. In front of each beach house before Zavala's, they stopped and sang Christmas carols. When her clear soprano joined in, it really brought it to life. The owners came out, offered punch and apple fritters at one house and orange sugar cookies at the next. Each stop drew out the owners of the next residence along the beach front.

At Zavala's, the last in the row, the pattern held. Zavala came out to hear them and brought a bottle of rum. On the last stretch of darkened beach, they knocked out his two guards with dart guns they'd stashed under the seats, drugged Zavala and his equally dangerous brother as well before tying them in back of the MRZRs, and continued on their way as if nothing had happened. His capture only took seconds.

Just inland was the little-used Aeródromo Capitán Eduardo Toledo. A small field used for tourist flights during the day, and nothing at night. The Chinook slipped in and they drove up the cargo bay ramp so fast that the helo barely stopped.

Once they were aloft and clear of Cozumel, Kelsey came to find him where he was leaning against the angle of the raised rear ramp—his normal post as tail gunner.

She still wore the hat.

And she opened her joined hands for just a moment to show that she still clutched the little packet of candy, before once more holding it to her chest. And her eyes, those wide, lovely eyes looked ready to take on the world.

Then she leaned in to kiss him. Not some quick thank you peck, but soft, lush, so full of warmth that for a moment he felt as if he was indeed lying on a sunny Cozumel beach with her.

"Thank you," she whispered from mere inches away.

Jason tried to come up with some quip. Something to ease the moment for the lady in the blinking Rudolph hat. But all he could think to whisper back was the same, "Thank *you*."

He'd assumed this Christmas would be hell, because of

the memories of the last one. Instead, she'd given him the gift of hope as a present.

When she kissed him again, this time letting herself curl up against him, he had hope for the many Christmases to come as well.

WILD JUSTICE (EXCERPT)

IF YOU LIKED THIS, YOU'LL LOVE DUANE AND SOFIA

WILD JUSTICE

(EXCERPT)

The low hill, shadowed by banana and mango trees in the twilight of the late afternoon sun above the Venezuelan jungle, overlooked the heavily guarded camp a half mile away. But that wasn't his immediate problem.

Right now, it took everything Duane Jenkins could do to ignore the stinging sweat dripping into his eyes. Any unwarranted motion or sound might attract his target's attention before he was in position.

From two meters away, he whispered harshly.

"Who the hell are you, sister? And how did you get here?"

"Holy crap!"

He couldn't help but smile. What kind of woman said *crap* when unexpectedly facing a sniper rifle at point-blank range?

"Not your sister," she gained points for a quick recovery. "Now get that rifle out of my face, Jarhead."

Ouch! That was low. He wasn't some damned, swamp-tromping Marine. Not even ex-Marine. He was ex-75th Rangers of the US Army, now two years in Delta Force. And as an operator for The Unit—as Delta called themselves—

that made him far superior to any other soldier no matter what the dudes in SEAL Team 6 thought about it. That also didn't explain who he'd just found here in *the* perfect sniper position overlooking General Raul Estevan Aguado's encampment.

It had taken him over fifteen hours to scout out this one perfect gap between the too-damn-tall trees that made up this sweaty place and, with just twenty meters to go, he'd spotted her heavily camouflaged form lying among the leaves. It had taken him another half hour to cover that distance without drawing her attention.

Where was a cold can of Coke when a guy needed one? This place was worse than Atlanta in the summer. The red earth had been driven so deep into his pores from crawling over the ground that he wondered if his skin color was permanently changed to rust red.

Why did evil bastards like Aguado have to come from such places?

More immediate problem, dude. Stay focused.

The woman's American English was accentless, sounding flat to his Southern ear. Probably from the Pacific Northwest or some other strange part of the country. But there was a thin overlay that matched her Latinate features—full-lipped with dark eyebrows and darker eyes, which was about all he could tell through her camo paint. The slight Spanish lilt shifted her to intriguingly exotic.

But she wasn't supposed to be here. No one was.

"Keeping you in my sights until I get some answers, ma'am," Duane kept his HK MSG90 A2 rifle aimed right at the bridge of her nose—a straight-through spine cutter if he had to take her down. It would be serious overkill, as the weapon was rated to lethal past eight hundred meters and they were whispering at each other from less than two meters apart. With the silencer, his weapon would be even quieter than their whispers, but he hadn't spent the last sixteen hours crawling into position to have her death cry give him away. If she so much as squawked as she went down, every goddamn bird in the jungle would light off, giving away his presence.

She sighed and nodded toward her own rifle that rested on the ground in front of her.

He shifted his focus—though not his aim—then let out a very low whistle of appreciation. A G28. Even his team hadn't gotten their hands on the latest entry into the US Army's sniper arsenal yet. Not quite the same accuracy as his own weapon but six inches shorter, several pounds lighter, and far more flexible to configure. A whole generational leap forward. Richie, his team's tech, would be geeking out right about now. The fact that he wasn't here to see it almost made Duane smile.

"A Heckler & Koch G28. What's your point, sister?" He drawled it out for Richie's sake, who'd be listening in on Duane's radio. Then the implications sank in. If his Delta Force team couldn't get these yet, then who could? Whatever else this woman was, she would be tied to one of the three US Special Mission Units: Delta, SEAL Team 6, or the combat controllers of the Air Force's 24th STS.

Or The Activity.

That fit.

The Intelligence Support Activity served the other three Special Mission Units. If she was with The Activity…that was seriously hot. It meant she was both one of the top intel specialists anywhere *and* a lethal fighter. And that meant that *she'd* been the one to put out the call that had brought him here and was sticking to see the job through. That at least answered why she was in his spot. It also said a lot that she hadn't taken any of several easier-to-reach locations that were almost as good.

"It is about time you caught a clue. Welcome to the conversation." She picked up her rifle as if his wasn't still aimed at her. Very chill. "You are being a little dense there, soldier." At least she got the *branch* of the military right this time.

"Hey, they don't call me 'The Rock' for nothing, darlin'," Duane lowered his barrel until it was pointed into the dirt. "They actually call me that becau—"

The moment his weapon was down, he suddenly was staring down the dark hole of the G28's silencer.

"Uh…"

"The Rock certainly isn't because you are a towering black movie star. It must be for your thick head."

Duane swallowed carefully, unable to shift his focus away from the barrel of her weapon to see if the safety was on or not.

"He spells his name differently. He's Dwayne 'The Rock' with a w and a y. I'm more normal, D-u-a-n-e T-h-e R-o-c-k." He made it sing-song just like the theme song from *The All-New Mickey Mouse Club* that he'd been hooked on as a little kid.

"M-o-u-s-e," she gave the appropriate response.

He couldn't help laughing, quietly, despite their positions —him still staring down the barrel of her weapon—because discovering Mickey Mouse in common in the heart of the Venezuelan jungle was just too funny.

"Normal is not what I need here," the woman sighed and there was the distinct click of her reengaging the safety on her rifle.

"Only thing normal about me is my name, ma'am." Always good to "ma'am" a woman with a sniper rifle pointed at your face.

"Prove it," she turned her weapon once more toward the camp half a kilometer away through the trees. Her motions were appropriately slow to not draw attention. However, it was too even a motion. A sniper learned to never break the pulses of nature's rhythm. She might be some hotshot intel agent—because The Activity absolutely rocked almost everything they did—but she still wasn't Delta, who rocked it all.

Duane breathed out slowly and spent the next couple minutes easing the last two meters toward her. Having the camp in view meant that one of their spotters could see them as well, if the bad guys were damned lucky. He and the woman both wore ghillie suits—that's why he'd gotten so close before he spotted her. The suits were made of open-weave cloth liberally decorated with leaves and twigs so that the two of them looked like little more than a patch of the jungle floor. He'd dragged his on backcountry jungle roads for twenty miles to make sure he smelled like the jungle as well. Having a jaguar trounce his ass wouldn't exactly brighten up his day.

Even their rifles were well camouflaged except for either end of the spotting scopes and the very tips of the barrels. If he hadn't recently been lusting over the new specs, he wouldn't have recognized her HK G28 at all in its disguise.

Getting into position as a sniper took a patience that only the most highly trained could achieve. A female sniper? That was a rare find indeed. The two women on his Delta team were damned fine shooters, but he and Chad were the snipers of the crew. A female sniper from The Activity? This just kept getting better and better. He'd pay a fair wage to know what she really looked like beneath the ghillie and all that face paint.

"Maybe you and I should go to the party as a couple." At long last he lay beside her, close enough that he would have felt her body heat if not for the smothering sauna of his ghillie suit.

"What party? And we're never going to be a couple."

"Halloween. It's only a couple weeks off. We could sneak in and nobody would see us in our ghillies. People would wonder why the punch bowls were mysteriously draining."

"And why the apples were bobbing on their own," she sounded disgusted. "What I want is—"

"Let's see what y'all are up to down there," he cut her off, just for the fun of it, and focused his rifle scope on the camp below. He was a little disappointed when there was no immediate comeback, though there was a low muttering in Spanish that he couldn't quite catch but it cheered his soul.

The general's camp was a simple affair in several ways. The enclosure was a few hundred meters across. An old-school fence of wooden stakes driven into the ground, each a small tree trunk three meters high with sharpened points upward. Not that the points mattered, because razor wire was looped along the top. Guard shacks every hundred meters—four total. The towers straddled the fence. Not a good idea. The structure should have been entirely behind the wall to protect it from attack. Unless…

"You got a name, darling?" Lying beside her, Duane could tell that she was shorter than he was. Her hands were fine, but her body was hidden by the ghillie so he couldn't read anything more about her looks.

"Yes, I have a name."

"That's nice. Always good to have yourself one of those," Duane could play that game just as well as the next person. He turned his attention to the camp. "Our friendly general isn't worried about attack from the outside or he'd have built his towers differently. He's worried about keeping people inside."

Sofia Forteza had already known that from her research, but she wondered how Duane—spelled the "normal" way—did.

She'd spent months tracking General Aguado. Cripes, she'd spent months finding him in the first place. He was a slippery *bastardo* who did most of his work through intermediaries and only rarely surfaced himself. Tracing him to this corner of the Guatopo National Park—so close to Caracas, the capital of Venezuela, that she'd dismissed it at first—had taken a month more.

Duane had taken one look at the place and seen…what?

He'd have built his towers differently.

She leaned back to her own scope and inspected them again. It took a moment to bring the towers into focus because her nerves were still zinging as if she'd been electrocuted. Somehow, in all her training, she'd never looked down the barrel of a rifle or even a handgun at point blank range—perhaps the scariest thing she'd ever seen.

Scariest other than Duane's cold blue eyes. He was the most dangerous-looking man she'd ever met, which is why his jokes and his smooth Southern accent were throwing her so badly. He sounded half badass, macho-bastard Unit operator and half southern gentleman. It was the strangest combination she'd ever heard. One moment he was wooing her with warm tones, obviously without a clue of how to woo a woman, and the next he was being pure Army grunt with a vocabulary to match. She simply couldn't figure him out.

Finally she shrugged her emotions aside enough to focus her scope properly. *Stay in the jungle, not in your head.* She rebuilt it in layers. The strange silence of the wind—not a single breath of air reached the jungle floor, instead it stagnated, adding to the oppressiveness of the heat. Macaw calls alternated between chatter and screech. Monkeys screamed and shouted in the upper branches. Buzzing flies had learned to leave her alone and the silent ants were no longer creeping her out. All that was left after she canceled each of those out was the man breathing beside her and the compound of that bastard Aguado that she'd been staring at for the last twenty-four hours.

The guard towers were supported by four long, tree-trunk legs, two inside the fence and two outside. Outside! Where they were vulnerable to attack. General Aguado hadn't built a fort in the depths of a national park—he'd built a prison.

All of her research had only uncovered his location, not his purpose here. Because she hadn't cared. Cutting the head off the snake one target at a time worked for her.

She looked again at the camp. Wooden shacks for the most part—workers' cabins. What else had she missed?

"Locks on the doors," Duane answered the question she hadn't asked in a whisper that was surprisingly soft for such a deep voice. He ignored a fer-de-lance pit viper as it slid up and over the ghillie covering his rifle barrel, slowing to inspect them with a flick of its tongue before continuing on its way in search of mice. If he could ignore the snake, so could she. Mostly. A little. She watched long after it had slithered out of sight.

Sofia looked at the shacks' doors again. Locks on the *outside*. She'd been watching the camp for twenty-four hours and had missed that. The dozens of armed guards weren't being lazy on patrol as she'd thought. They didn't care about the outside world—they were worried about the inside one. And because they were the only armed personnel in the camp, and everyone knew it, they could afford to be nonchalant.

Back to the towers. The guards were leaning on the inside rails looking down, not the outside ones looking out. All of her work to slip into this position was probably meaningless. If Duane was right, she could walk right up and knock on the front gate before anyone would pay her the least attention. A band of red howler monkeys working their way noisily through the jungle canopy above the camp didn't even attract a glance from the guards.

Still, Aguado was here. She'd seen him arrive with his entourage. And he was never going to leave. Not alive.

"Not a nice place," Duane observed quietly.

"Not a nice man."

"Sure I am. You just don't know me yet, sugar."

Sofia brought her knee up sharply. Lying side by side, she was able to bullseye the Charlie-horse nerve cluster on his outer thigh. Her nana hadn't raised her to be a target.

"Shit!" He didn't sound so almighty pleased with himself any longer, though he did manage to keep it to a whisper as he continued swearing.

Why did guys always think they were so charming? With her looks, she should be used to it by now. Except her looks were hidden by the ghillie suit. What had kicked Duane-spelled-the-normal-way into such a guy mode? Just that she was female? When did Delta start recruiting cavemen as their standard? Actually, that one she knew the answer to—since Day One if past experience meant anything.

She hadn't ever deployed with Delta before, but she'd met enough of them to know the type. They were the rebel super-warriors of the US military. Everyone thought that their team was the baddest, but Delta Force, more commonly called "The Unit," completely owned that title. Somehow they drew the people that didn't fit anywhere else in the military. But where they'd been troublemakers in their old units, 1st Special Forces Operational Detachment-Delta collected them and honed their skills. They were like a barely controlled reaction just bubbling along, waiting for an excuse to explode.

"So, what's the general's story?" Duane, once he was done nursing his thigh, went for a subject change proving he wasn't stupid.

"Deep in the drug trade. Known to have called for at least three high profile murders, including a Supreme Tribunal of Justice judge (that's their version of the Supreme Court) even if he didn't pull the trigger himself."

"Oh, so *he's* the one that's not nice," as if Duane only now was figuring that out.

She was not going to be charmed by him. His every tone said that just because she was female, he'd switched into some weird-ass flirt mode. She'd had enough of that coming up through the ranks to last a lifetime.

"This isn't slave labor, so you'd better add human trafficking to your list." With the speed of a light switch, all the charm was gone from Duane's voice.

As if to prove his point, at that moment a couple of guards exited a small building, readjusting their pants and laughing. They kicked the door shut behind them and snapped the lock closed. No question what they'd just been doing to some poor women—one of the perks of their job.

Numerous guards. Locks on the outside of the cabin doors. No large central building that might be an illicit drug lab or slave labor textile sweatshop. This was a holding pen, hidden deep in the jungle of a national park. The few people who were circulating around, aside from the guards, were almost all women. Women who were keeping their heads down and trudging about their tasks. The sickness that twisted in her stomach had nothing to do with lying still for the last twenty-four hours.

Sofia wasn't even aware of raising her rifle until Duane reached over and casually pushed it back down.

"Not yet." It was all he said, but she could hear the anger beneath the soft words.

Well that wasn't shit compared to what *she* was feeling at the moment. This place needed to be erased from the map. Scorched to the ground, removed permanently from existence!

"Why are you here? I sent for a goddamn team, not some Southern Rock."

He flashed a smile at her, "If you've got me, you don't need a team." All of his macho bravado was back. As if she'd misheard his momentary anger. He sounded too much like her useless brother and the rest of her useless family. She couldn't be rid of him fast enough.

As the last of the sunlight faded from the sky and the bird calls tapered toward silence, Sofia wondered who she was going to want to shoot more by sunrise: General Raul Estevan Aguado or Duane The Rock?

Available at fine retailers everywhere!
Wild Justice

ABOUT THE AUTHOR

M.L. Buchman started the first of, what is now over 50 novels and as many short stories, while flying from South Korea to ride his bicycle across the Australian Outback. Part of a solo around the world trip that ultimately launched his writing career.

All three of his military romantic suspense series—The Night Stalkers, Firehawks, and Delta Force—have had a title named "Top 10 Romance of the Year" by the American Library Association's *Booklist.* NPR and Barnes & Noble have named other titles "Top 5 Romance of the Year." In 2016 he was a finalist for Romance Writers of America prestigious RITA award. He also writes: contemporary romance, thrillers, and fantasy.

Past lives include: years as a project manager, rebuilding and single-handing a fifty-foot sailboat, both flying and jumping out of airplanes, and he has designed and built two houses. He is now making his living as a full-time writer on the Oregon Coast with his beloved wife and is constantly amazed at what you can do with a degree in Geophysics. You may keep up with his writing and receive a free starter e-library by subscribing to his newsletter at: www.mlbuchman.com

Other works by M. L. Buchman:

<u>The Night Stalkers</u>
MAIN FLIGHT
The Night Is Mine
I Own the Dawn
Wait Until Dark
Take Over at Midnight
Light Up the Night
Bring On the Dusk
By Break of Day
WHITE HOUSE HOLIDAY
Daniel's Christmas
Frank's Independence Day
Peter's Christmas
Zachary's Christmas
Roy's Independence Day
Damien's Christmas
AND THE NAVY
Christmas at Steel Beach
Christmas at Peleliu Cove
5E
Target of the Heart
Target Lock on Love
Target of Mine

<u>Firehawks</u>
MAIN FLIGHT
Pure Heat
Full Blaze
Hot Point
Flash of Fire
Wild Fire
SMOKEJUMPERS
Wildfire at Dawn
Wildfire at Larch Creek
Wildfire on the Skagit

<u>Delta Force</u>
Target Engaged
Heart Strike
Wild Justice

<u>Where Dreams</u>
Where Dreams are Born
Where Dreams Reside
Where Dreams Are of Christmas
Where Dreams Unfold
Where Dreams Are Written

<u>Eagle Cove</u>
Return to Eagle Cove
Recipe for Eagle Cove
Longing for Eagle Cove
Keepsake for Eagle Cove

<u>Henderson's Ranch</u>
Nathan's Big Sky

<u>Love Abroad</u>
Heart of the Cotswolds: England

<u>Dead Chef Thrillers</u>
Swap Out!
One Chef!
Two Chef!

<u>Deities Anonymous</u>
Cookbook from Hell: Reheated
Saviors 101

<u>SF/F Titles</u>
The Nara Reaction
Monk's Maze
the Me and Elsie Chronicles

<u>Strategies for Success (NF)</u>
Managing Your Inner Artist/Writer
Estate Planning for Authors